Dimanche Diller at Sea

Dimanche Diller at Sea

Henrietta Branford

Illustrated by
Emma Chichester-Clark

CollinsChildren'sBooks
An imprint of HarperCollins*Publishers*

The lines quoted on page 61 are from *Sweet and Low*
by Alfred, Lord Tennyson.

First published in Great Britain by Collins 1996
1 3 5 7 9 10 8 6 4 2

Collins is an imprint of HarperCollins*Publishers* Ltd,
77-85 Fulham Palace Road, Hammersmith, London W6 8JB.

Text copyright © Henrietta Branford 1996
Illustrations copyright © Emma Chichester-Clark 1996

ISBN 0 00 675145-8

Printed and bound in Great Britain by Caledonian International
Book Manufacturing Ltd, Glasgow, G64

For Norah East,
my more-than-Godmother

One

Dimanche Diller woke up suddenly. Moonlight streamed in through her open window. Her bedroom was tucked under the eaves of Hilton Hall, directly below the attic, and she could feel the silence of the empty rooms all round her. She got up, leaned her elbows on the windowsill, and pushed her curly dark hair out of her eyes. Everything was still and quiet. Everything felt perfectly normal ... or as normal as things do, by night.

Somewhere in Monks Wood a dog barked. Down in the village a door banged. The milk train clanked towards Rockford Market. These were the familiar night noises of the Hilton Valley and they had not woken Dimanche. No. Something quieter, something nearer, had crept into her sleeping mind and whispered *danger*.

Although she was only ten years old, Dimanche had already lived a more adventurous life than many people ever do. She had lost both her parents in a storm at sea when she was just a tiny baby, and had fallen into the hands of Valburga Vilemile, a woman who was both cruel and cunning. Valburga had done her best to make Dimanche's early life unhappy. Once or twice, driven by greed for Dimanche's inheritance, she had even tried to bring about her death.

Imprisoned in a dank dark cellar, trapped in a burning building, hypnotised and held to ransom, Dimanche had developed a sixth sense for danger. Although she had now lived for some time in happiness and safety, cared for by her aunt, Verity Victorine, that sixth sense never slumbered and it woke her now.

She pulled a dressing gown on over her nightie and crept onto the landing. From there she could see all along the corridor to the bottom of the attic stairs, and down the main staircase into the hall. No one was visible.

A puddle of silver spilled in from the fanlight over the large front door and lit each crack and cranny in the stone-flagged floor. Beyond, the old house dreamt in darkness. Dimanche tiptoed down the stairs. Everything was exactly as it ought to be. Except that the door to Verity Victorine's study was open.

Perhaps you feel Dimanche should have gone back to bed at this point? Or at the very least, woken her aunt. You may be right, but she did neither. Instead, she took a deep breath, pushed open the door, and walked in.

Although the little room was empty, Dimanche could tell that someone had been there only seconds earlier. A damp smell, rather like toadstools, tainted the air, and the window, which Verity usually closed before going to bed, was open. As Dimanche looked out at the moonlit garden, a dark shape caught her eye.

A tall, thin man was standing by the yew hedge. His head was bent, and his face was hidden in deep shadow, but somehow Dimanche knew that if she could have seen it, she would not have liked it.

As Dimanche watched, the man raised his head and stared straight at her.

She saw that she had been right about his face. You may have seen one like it, somewhere. It was the kind that says: *Me first. You don't matter. In fact, you don't exist.*

9

It was the kind of face that can only belong to someone very, very selfish. Feeling suddenly afraid, Dimanche moved back until the curtain hid her. She glanced over her shoulder to make sure there was nobody behind her.

When she looked back into the garden, the thin man had gone.

Two

"Do you think you left the study window open last night?" Dimanche asked her aunt, the next morning.

"No, I'm sure I didn't. Why?"

"I woke up and thought I heard a noise. I went downstairs to see if anyone was there, and found the study window open. There was a musty smell, like toadstools. And I thought I saw—"

"*Dimanche*! You *shouldn't* have! Gone downstairs, I mean. You should have woken me!"

A loud thump, followed by an angry yowl from Cyclops, the Hilton Hall cat, announced the arrival of the morning post on the doormat.

"You'd think he'd know by now not to sit there, wouldn't you?" Dimanche said, glad of a chance to change the subject. "Shall I fetch the post?"

"Do, Dimanche."

Verity Victorine was a nun. She belonged to the Order of Sainte Gracieuse in Normandy, and had lived peacefully in a small French convent until the day she discovered that Dimanche needed her help. At once she left the convent and hurried back to Hilton Hall, but she still exchanged letters and small gifts with the sisters almost daily.

Verity Victorine loved getting letters. Who does not? But this particular post brought her no pleasure. Her forehead, usually calm and smooth beneath her clean white coif, criss-crossed itself with worry lines and her hands shook as she read her letter for the third time. She stirred marmalade into her hot chocolate, and dropped her letter in a pool of melted butter.

"Is something wrong, Aunt Verity?"

"Read this, Dimanche."

The letter Verity handed to Dimanche was hand-written on expensive paper. This is what it said:

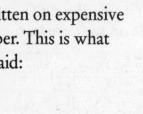

Friday, 22nd June.

Dear Madam,
Every one hundred years, on Midsummer Midnight, the
Reigning Sovereign calls upon a Lawyer of this county to
inspect and ratify the Diller Deed and Title.

This century it's us – Bludgeon & Bludgeon.

We therefore plan to call upon you to inspect the said
Deed and Title, with customary hospitality of a Hogshead
of Brandy, on Midsummer Midnight. We beg to remind
you that the Ancient Proclamation was laid down by King
William the First in the Royal Domesday Book of 1086
and that no Diller has ever failed to obey it.

Your Obedient Servants,
Baldwin and Bartholomew Bludgeon.

PS Should Miss Diller fail to present the Deed and Title,
then everything – House, Hall, Woods, Goods, Serfs,
Chattels, and Appurtenances – including children – must
pass into the hand of whomever else may do so.

Dimanche tossed the letter down. "Don't worry, Aunt Verity," she said, "I know all about the Deed and Title."

"Do you, Dimanche? I had quite forgotten it. I don't even know where it is. I suppose I shall have to tidy my desk." Verity Victorine sighed. Sometimes she longed for the quiet of the convent.

"Don't worry, Aunt Verity, it isn't in your desk. It's in a strongbox in the bank at Rockford Market."

The little furrows beneath Verity's white coif vanished, and she poured herself a second cup of chocolate, this time without marmalade.

"Dimanche, you're a marvel! How do you *know*?"

"There's a chest in the attic, Aunt Verity, it's full of family papers. I opened it once, when I was looking for a penknife, and read some of them. One was from Great-grandfather Darius, the last Diller to present the Deed and Title for inspection. He wrote down where it's kept, and what it looks like, and what you have to do with it, so that the next Diller to do it – me – would know."

"That's that, then, Dimanche," said Verity, happily.

Unfortunately, it wasn't.

Three

Beyond the summer meadow, Polly Cockle's kitchen window caught the morning sun, and winked. Dimanche smiled as Polly left her cottage and crossed the meadow, stopping now and then to enjoy the flowers that grew beside the path.

Polly had come to Hilton Hall during the dark days of Valburga Vilemile's rule, to be Dimanche's nanny. She had arrived on Dimanche's third birthday, and until the day that Verity Victorine arrived, and Valburga Vilemile departed, she never left Dimanche's side. They even took their holidays together, pony trekking in the New Forest, and rock climbing on the beautiful island of Skye. They had been through victory and defeat together, and they were more than ordinary friends.

Polly's husband, Cosmo Cockle, was the gardener at Hilton Hall. He, too, was a true friend to Dimanche, and often brought her little presents – a bunch of earthy carrots, a yellow pear, and once, a mysterious pupa that Dimanche kept in a jar until the creature within was ready to emerge and fly free. When Polly and Cosmo were married in the church at Hilton in the Hollow, Dimanche was their bridesmaid.

Polly smiled hello to Verity and Dimanche as she came into the kitchen. Dimanche poured her a cup of hot chocolate and passed her the *Rockford Record*.

"Will you listen to this!" Polly exclaimed, after a moment's reading.

RAIDERS ROB ROCKFORD WHILE CITIZENS SLUMBER!
"IT'S CRIMINAL!" SAYS CHAUNCEY COIN.

Thieves broke in last night and robbed the bank in Rockford Market Square. Valuable old documents have gone astray.

Dimanche and Verity turned suddenly pale.

... "This is the first time in the history of our little bank that we have sustained a loss due to criminal activity," said distressed Manager Chauncey Coin, fifty-year-old grandfather of seven. "Fire we've suffered. Flood too, when the Fenny burst its banks in 1855. But crime? Never!"

"Dimanche! Verity!" Polly cried. "Whatever is the matter?"
Verity phoned the bank at once, and Chauncey Coin confirmed her worst fears.

The Diller Deed was gone. Barely ten minutes later, Verity, Polly and Dimanche were bumping anxiously along between dusty summer hedges on the Rockford Market bus.

Four

Brother Betony stood on the bridge in Monks Wood and stared down into the peat brown swirls and dimples of the Fenny.

His black robe seemed to drift around him in the early evening air. He leaned his elbows on the wooden railing and rested his pale face on his pale hands.

Upstream he could see the grey stones of the ruined Abbey, half-hidden by green bracken. Downstream, trees and more trees wove a leafy border to the sky. In one of them – it was an ancient yew – someone had carved a heart into the bark around the letters *B* and *B*.

A vixen trotted over the bridge. For all the notice that she took of Brother Betony, he might have been part of the parapet.

Next, Dimanche appeared on the path. Brother Betony watched her for a moment with a smile on his old face. He straightened himself slowly, and his black robe brushed soundlessly against the wooden railings of the bridge. An old wound pinched at the top of his backbone. He raised a pale hand to the back of his neck to ease the stiffness there, and faded slowly into the golden evening light.

Dimanche sat down on the bridge and dangled her legs over the edge. She ran over the day's events in her mind. The visit to the bank had upset Sister Verity dreadfully, though Chauncey Coin had been both kind and helpful. The police had been sent for, and Chief Superintendent Barry Bullpit was on his way. There was nothing to be done but wait, Aunt Verity had said.

Dimanche did not agree. She stood up as the sun began to set and made her way out of Monks Wood as fast as she could. She did not want to be there alone, when darkness filled the silent space between the trees. Already the wood lapped round her like deep water. Beyond lay open country. A fallow deer, making for the fields to fill its belly with soft grass, startled Dimanche with a sudden cough.

Hawthorn hedges criss-crossed the little valley, turning it into a giant's chess board. Beside a deep pool of the Fenny, an old stone boathouse caught the light, and shone. On any other summer evening, Dimanche might have stopped to launch the raft she kept there, but tonight there wasn't time. She must reach the old quarry before dark.

The quarry was a disused chalk pit, hollowed out of the side of a hill. Protected from winter storms by a white cliff left by the extraction of the chalk, it looked across the wide sweep of the Fenny valley to the south and west. Private and secluded, this was the regular stopping place of Papa Fettler. The old barn, which had once held sacks of chalk, now made a stable for his pony. A spring rose nearby, providing drinking water, cold and clear, and very slightly bubbly. Papa Fettler had built a small round well, conveniently placed, and kept a cup and bucket handy.

"Will you take a drop of my champagne?" he would ask Dimanche, when she called to see him there. Dimanche would take the tin mug, and dip, sip, and relish the clean taste.

Papa Fettler's home was a battered caravan. He travelled where fancy took him, and stopped where evening found him, and you could never be sure where that might be, but the quarry was a good place to look. On this particular evening Dimanche was very glad to find him there.

"Well, Miss Dimanche," he remarked, as she came panting round the bend of the cart track. "You look proper rattled. Will you take a bowl of mushroom soup? Or perhaps you'd like a dandelion salad?"

Dimanche shook her head. "No thanks, I'm not hungry, Papa Fettler. And anyway there isn't time."

"No time for supper? Why not, Miss Dimanche?"

"Something awful's happened, Papa Fettler, and we may all have to leave the Hilton Valley – even you!"

"I doubt that, Miss Dimanche. There's been Dillers at the Hall these many hundred years, and Fettlers in the Hollow. What's got you flustered?"

Dimanche sat down, gulped a mug of blackberry leaf tea, and told Papa Fettler, as quickly as she could, about the letter from Bludgeon & Bludgeon, and the break-in, and the thin man in the garden, and lastly about the theft of the Diller Deed and Title from the Rockford Market bank.

"What are we going to do, Papa Fettler? What *are* we going to *do*?"

Papa Fettler emptied out his pipe, unblocked the stem with a quill, scraped out the bowl with a little brass scraper, recharged it with tobacco from his leather pouch, and lit it with a spill from the fire. When at last he replied, it was with a question.

"Do you know the story of Benedicta, Miss Dimanche?"

Dimanche shook her head.

"Then I'll tell it to you. It's a good story, and if you're in trouble, you'd best know it. Listen."

Dimanche settled herself beside the fire, and tried not to fidget.

"Benedicta was a wise woman," Papa Fettler began. "Lived in Monks Wood five hundred years ago. She used to cure sick people, when she could. The villagers brought her bread and eggs and ale and suchlike, in return.

"One afternoon, just on Midsummer – hot it was, like now, with the bees buzzing, and the Fenny splash-splashing, and the birds a-dozing on the twig – a woman brought her child to Benedicta to be cured of a fever."

Papa Fettler shook his head, as though remembering. He looked at Dimanche from under the brim of his wide hat, and his grey eyes seemed to see again all that he described to her. His battered brown face took on a sad and sorrowful fold of feature as he gazed into the little fire glow.

"It was hot, like I said. Hot, and still, with the trees hanging over the Fenny like great green cabbages, and the air a-shimmer, and the fish down deep."

The sound of Papa Fettler's voice grew faint and distant. Behind and underneath it, Dimanche could hear water lap-lapping, and heavy foliage rustling to a summer breeze, and a tired baby crying.

"The woman put her child on Benedicta's lap and stole away. Everyone knew that Benedicta liked to do her healing alone. She used to say the healing power flowed strongest that way, but it's my belief that people's conversation bored her, so she sent 'em packing. Babies was what she liked. Ought to have had a bundle of her own, but that's another story. She loved a monk, you see, name of Betony. A poor choice from Benedicta's point of view, because he was sworn to celibacy, and could never marry. He was a good man, see, and would not break his vows.

"Well, the child dropped into sweet sleep in an instant. And there's nothing makes a body feel more somnolent than to have a baby fall asleep on 'em, Miss Dimanche. Nothing. It's the little wheeze and snuffle that they make, and the weight of their limbs as they give their body up to restfulness. Well. Benedicta smiled down at the child. 'You're cured already, you are,' she said. 'You must have been just on the turn.'

"And with that, she shut her eyes, and fell asleep herself. And there they was, wise woman and wise baby, asleep in the shade by the banks of the Fenny."

Dimanche found her own eyes closing. Against her eyelids, patterns of green leaves danced, splashed by trembling river light.

"Well. That was long ago." Papa Fettler sighed, a sad and sorrowful sigh.

"What was? What happened, Papa Fettler?"

"The woman slept. The baby slept. A wolf came out of the wood. When the woman awoke, the baby was gone. There was nothing but a paw print in the damp margin of the Fenny to say where it had gone."

Dimanche opened her eyes and sat up. The sound of running and crying, of weeping and anger and lamentation, filled her ears, then faded.

"How horrible. How absolutely horrible."

Papa Fettler nodded.

"And there was worse to follow, nearly. Nearly, but not quite. The baby's mother wanted Benedicta burned for a witch. Fetched up the faggots herself. But the village people wouldn't have it. In the end, that poor mother came to her senses – revenge is nothing but a poison, Miss Dimanche, and when once the worst of her despair was past, she knew it. But Benedicta never forgave herself. Not properly. She took to living all alone in a cave and ate nothing but fish, to which she was powerfully averse, until her dying day."

Silence filled the little quarry. Dimanche felt as though she'd just returned to it from somewhere else entirely.

"What a sad old story, Papa Fettler."

"But there's one last part to it, Miss Dimanche, that ain't sad, and that's the part that concerns you. *That baby was a Diller.* That baby was your great-great-many-times-great aunt. And Benedicta took an oath, after that baby died. She took a solemn oath to come to the aid of any Diller, then or in time to come, if ever Dillers were in direst need. And they do say that her powers are at their strongest around Midsummer."

Dimanche felt bitterly disappointed. She had expected Papa Fettler to tell her something useful.

"I don't see how she can help me, Papa Fettler. Not if she's been dead for hundreds of years."

Papa Fettler smiled. "Who sees everything there is to see?" he asked. "You'd best go on home now, your poor aunt will be all of a lather. Tomorrow we may see if Benedicta keeps her promise."

Six

When Dimanche got in, she found her aunt sitting at the kitchen table, dabbing at her eyes with the corner of a soft cotton pillowcase. It was one of a set of twelve she was embroidering for the Sisters of Sainte Gracieuse. She picked up her needle, pricked her finger with it, put it down again, and smiled in a distracted way at Dimanche.

"I hoped that some sewing might calm me, Dimanche, but it hasn't. How can I ever forgive myself?"

"It's not *your* fault, Aunt Verity! You weren't to know someone would rob the bank!"

"I am your guardian, Dimanche. I feel responsible. What can I do?"

"I think you ought to go to bed, Aunt Verity. You look tired out."

"I am, my child. But what about your supper?"

"I'll make myself a sandwich. Would you like one too?"

Verity shook her head. "I couldn't eat,

Dimanche. I'll take a drop of the peach brandy to settle my stomach."

Dimanche made herself a sandwich of Swiss cheese with watercress, and another of peanut butter with thin slices of cucumber. Then she fetched the peach brandy and poured her aunt a thimbleful. She carried it carefully up the broad, dark stairs, and tapped quietly on her aunt's bedroom door. No reply. She peeped in.

Sister Verity was sleeping soundly in her big four-poster bed. Dimanche tiptoed over, put the tiny glass of peach brandy down on the bedside table, and kissed her aunt goodnight. Verity smiled in her sleep but did not wake as Dimanche crept quietly out and closed the bedroom door behind her.

There is a place in every house where the air is cold, and the shadows are dark, and the bravest person feels afraid without quite knowing why. The foot of the attic stairs was that place in Hilton Hall. Dimanche had disliked it for as long as she could remember.

But up in the attic was the family letter chest, which held Great-grandfather Darius Diller's notebooks. Dimanche had glanced at them once before. One of them, she was almost certain, mentioned Benedicta's cave, and a hidden island. If Benedicta was to help her, Dimanche knew she must find out as much as possible about the hermit's life. She would start in the attic.

Once, when Dimanche was very little, Valburga Vilemile had locked her in the attic as a punishment for accidentally spilling her milk on the carpet. Dimanche had spent an afternoon of terror there, until Cosmo Cockle, at work in the flower bed below, heard her small sobs, and rescued her.

It's an inconvenient fact that the nastiest things that happen to you are often the hardest to forget. As she approached the attic stairs, Dimanche remembered exactly how it had felt to be pulled roughly up those stairs and pushed in through that door, to hear the key turn in the lock behind her, to listen to Valburga's cruel laugh, and to hear her footsteps fading.

She stood still at the bottom of the attic stairs, gathering her courage. "Those days are gone," she told herself. "Valburga cannot hurt me now."

A soft, grey layer of dust powdered the wooden staircase, and a musty odour tickled her nose. As her eyes got used to the shadows, Dimanche saw footsteps in the dust, the edge of each print etched clear and sharp against the polished oak treads. They led up to the attic door. And they did not come back down.

Dimanche wanted very much to run back to her sleeping aunt, wake her up, show her the footsteps, and let *her* decide what should be done about them. But then she thought about Verity's tired face asleep upon her pillow, and she couldn't bring herself to do it. Instead she forced herself, step by shaking step, up those dark stairs.

Old houses breathe at night. They creak, and tick, and rustle. Dimanche knew this, but every soft sound made her jump. Nevertheless, she lifted the latch, and pushed open the door.

A finger of moonlight slid in through the little dormer window and groped across the dusty floor.

Boxes and bags lined the room. A broken clock stared silently at Dimanche, its white face blank and still. A basket full of mousetraps glinted in a corner. A stuffed otter with glass eyes glared down from the wall.

The dormer window blew softly open; the sugary scent of wisteria blossom floated on the summer air. A moth drifted in, drunk with nectar, and drifted out again. A hunting bat swept close to the wall of the house and took the moth with a tiny squeak of triumph.

Why was the window open? Dimanche turned to scan the attic. There was no one there. Whoever had come up the attic stairs, leaving their footprints in the dust, must have left by the window and climbed down the thick coils of the wisteria.

She shone her torch onto the letter chest. Letters and notebooks spilled from it, higgledy-piggledy, across the floor. The prints of two large hands with long, thin fingers showed clearly on the lid.

Dimanche gathered up her parents' letters to each other first – fond letters full of plans and ending with *I-love-you's*, that had made her cry herself to sleep when first she read them. She bundled them neatly together and put them carefully back into the chest.

Now for Great-grandfather Darius's notebooks, she thought.

But his notebooks were gone.

Seven

Dimanche scribbled a note to Verity Victorine, in case she should wake in the night. *Gone out*, it said, *but am probably safe. Love, Dimanche.* Then she hurried off into the summer night to look for Wolfie T. Volfango.

Wolfie was Dimanche's closest friend. He lived alone, deep in the woods of Hilton in the Hollow. He had to. He was on the run.

Wolfie looked rather like a bear. His head was round and bald. His eyes were tiny. His craggy jaw jutted out over his barrel chest like the prow of a ship. His shoulders were massive, and his arms were long and powerful, with huge hands on the ends of them. His legs were short and strong. His smile, though shy, was warm and welcoming. But the strangest thing about him was his passion, his deep longing, his urgent *need* to fly. Wolfie was absolutely crazy about planes. Every second of his spare time was spent in designing them. Every ounce of his spare energy was spent in trying to build them. One day, he knew, he would succeed.

Strange stories were whispered in the bar of the Hilton Handshake on winter nights, when the inn sign creaked and the wind howled round the chimney pots. Stories of a mysterious man who roamed the woods and fields, foraging for food, and building weird contraptions. Folk sometimes caught a glimpse of him at sunset, on top of Steepdown Hill, gazing longingly up into the wide, wild sky.

On the whole, the villagers were content to leave him in peace. "He's done no harm to us nor ours," they'd say. "Give us a pint of Hilton Valley Velvet and we'll drink his health." And that would be that.

All the same, Wolfie was not the sort of friend you could arrange to meet just anywhere. Some time previously, he had fallen foul of the law, and Chief Superintendent Barry Bullpit had never closed his case. Wolfie seldom bivouacked in the same place for two nights in a row.

Dimanche had been walking in the woods for a good hour before the warm smell of baked potatoes and melting cheese told her that she was getting close to Wolfie. She gave an owl hoot, to let him know that it was her, and he returned their signal.

Soon Dimanche saw a familiar figure bending over a small wood fire. His mighty hunter hat was pushed well back, and the firelight danced on his bald head.

"Wolfie!" she cried. "Thank goodness I've found you!"

"Is something wrong, Dimanche? I was just goin' to have supper."

"You eat, Wolfie. I'll explain."

When Dimanche got to the part about Benedicta and the baby, Wolfie stopped eating, and wiped his nose on his sleeve.

"I wish you never told me that part, Dimanche," he said. "It makes me want to bawl. To think of that little baby, not doing nothing to nobody, and a great big wolf comes up and eats it. It wouldn't even know what it was being et by."

"It's awful, Wolfie, isn't it? But because of that poor baby, Benedicta made a promise. She promised to help any Diller, then or in time to come, if we should be in trouble."

"I don't think an old dead woman is gonna be much help, Dimanche. She didn't ought to make a promise that she couldn't keep."

"I know, Wolfie. But we've got to try."

"I guess it won't hurt to look for her cave, Dimanche."

"I knew you'd understand, Wolfie."

"First thing tomorrow morning, Dimanche."

"Now, Wolfie. Listen." The church clock was striking twelve. "That means we've got exactly twenty-four hours until Midsummer Midnight."

"Dimanche, it's dark."

"The moon'll be up in a minute, Wolfie. I'm sure the cave is somewhere in Monks Wood, I remember that much from my great-grandfather's notebook. And I bet it wasn't far from the river, because of all that fishing. We'll search both banks."

"I don't want to find no dead woman, Dimanche. And I don't want to find no wolves neither."

"There aren't any wolves left in England, Wolfie."

"Shucks, that's no comfort, Dimanche. They didn't ought to have killed 'em all. That wolf was only bein' a wolf."

Dimanche sighed. Sometimes it was hard to explain things properly to Wolfie.

"Try not to think about it," she advised.

One hour later, dirty and cold and wet from clambering along the river bank, hair full of twigs and legs all splashed with mud, Dimanche and Wolfie stopped for a short rest. A little wind made the trees whine, and wrapped ragged clouds around the moon. A flicker of lightning shot across the sky, followed by a growl of thunder.

"How much longer are we gonna carry on for, Dimanche? I don't fancy gettin' struck by lightnin'. And there's a funny smell round here."

"We'll carry on down to the old yew tree, Wolfie, then we'll stop and rest. There must be toadstools growing near here."

"Fools!" muttered a tall, thin man, who watched them from behind a tree. "Inconvenient, interfering idiots!" Like Wolfie, he was hiding out in Monks Wood. He would have preferred a place by the fire at the Hilton Handshake, but he did not wish his presence to be known in the village. Not yet. He did not see the monk on the bridge, who watched him watching them.

When Wolfie and Dimanche got up to carry on with their search, the thin man followed them. He was still following them when, one long hour later, they collapsed, famished and exhausted, on a mossy bank under the giant yew tree. High up among the branches someone had carved the letters *B* and *B*, and drawn a wobbly heart round them.

Deep down, below Wolfie's sleepy body, the great tree grasped the earth, roots delving far down beneath the pillows of soft moss. Brambles threw out their prickled arms and stiff, dry bracken, two metres tall and sharp as swords, pushed through the summer's growth.

A low mound of freshly dug earth spilling down the bank caught Wolfie's eye. He knelt to look for paw prints in the soft soil. Delicately, with his stubby fingers, he plucked a few strands of grey hair from a bramble.

"Wolves," he murmured excitedly to Dimanche.

"Badgers," she murmured back.
Leaning forwards to look into the
opening of the sett, she rested her
hand against a fallen branch.
The wood cracked and gave
way. Dimanche tumbled
forwards and disappeared.

Eight

Deep down, inky, lightless, sightless dark wrapped round Dimanche. The musty smell of underground blotted out what other smells there might have been. The splashing of the Fenny, the breeze in the trees, the roosting birds, all died. Dimanche heard Wolfie stumbling round up on the bank above her head. She heard his "Ouch!" as a bramble caught his ear. She heard a thump and a thud. After that, nothing. Summer thunder reverberated overhead. Each time Dimanche's eyes began to grow accustomed to the dark, a flash of lightning blinded her.

"Wolfie?" she called. "Where are you?" There was no reply.

Slowly the peals of thunder died away, and the wind tore a hole in the clouds. The moon sailed into it and hung there like a ship in a lagoon. The sky behind it turned a watery green, and a wash of silver light revealed the flight of ancient steps down which Dimanche had fallen. She stood up, rubbing her bruised bits, and looked about.

She saw that she was in a cave which had been hollowed out inside the mossy bank under the giant yew tree. It was about the size of a smallish bedroom. The ceiling was held up by a web of tree roots, and the floor was smooth and dry. A soft, mysterious glow, warmer than moonlight, was welling down the steps.

An old man appeared against the sky, his round head haloed by the moon. He carried a lantern in his hand and was bending forwards to look down into the cave. Although his face was smooth and unmarked by time, Dimanche felt that he was very old. Older than Tom Shovel the gravedigger. Older than Papa Fettler. Older than the oldest person she had ever seen. The light from his lantern fell onto her upturned face and painted her freckles yellow. Dimanche smiled up into the ancient face, and Brother Betony smiled down.

"I see you have found Benedicta's cave," he said. His voice was as airy as a puff of smoke.

"Have I?" asked Dimanche. "Can you see my friend Wolfie up there? Is he all right?"

"Your friend is safe, Dimanche."

The old man came slowly down the steps towards Dimanche. She felt a moment of fear as his pale, frail hands stretched down to her, but when their fingers touched she felt lightness and ease wrap round her.

"You know my name. But who are you?"

"My name is Brother Betony. I have known you for a long time, Dimanche. You, and your name, and all your family."

"Did you know my mother and my father?"

"And their parents. And their parents' parents."

"Then you must be ..."

"Very old."

Silence fell between Dimanche and Brother Betony. Dimanche noticed the strange, home-made sandals he wore on his otherwise bare brown feet. She noticed his home-made belt, and the strange, coarse cloth his robe was made of. Everything he wore looked home-made. Nothing he had could possibly have come from a shop.

"Are you a ghost, Brother Betony?" she asked.

"I am a shadow. An echo. A swirl in the river of time that washes through this ancient wood."

Dimanche touched the old man's hand where it lay, so light she could almost see through it to the folds of his black robe. His skin felt warm and dry.

"Was it you who Benedicta loved?"

"It was."

"Why didn't you stop being a monk and marry her?"

"Because I had taken my vows, before ever I saw her face." He sighed, and the yew tree rustled sadly overhead. "Your friend Wolfie will think you've turned into a spirit too, Dimanche. We must go and put his mind at rest." He led her up the steps and out through tall green bracken.

The sight of Dimanche appearing out of the ground hand in hand with a strange looking monk did not immediately put Wolfie's mind at rest. He looked from Dimanche to Brother Betony and back again.

"Are you . . .?" he began. "Is he . . .? Someone must of hit me. Must have shook my brain up. Because I think I'm seein' ghosts."

"You are, Wolfie," Dimanche told him.

Brother Betony nodded. "I am the ghost of

Monks Wood, Wolfie. I perished by the sword these many years ago."

"I n-never met no one who perished by the sword," Wolfie stammered. "Did it hurt?"

"It was a quick death. Now, children, listen to me. Once you leave this wood, I cannot help you. But Benedicta can. Go down into her cave, Dimanche, and wait there till she sends you word."

"Just me? Can't Wolfie come with me?"

"Wolfie will stay with me. There is the small matter of his head to attend to. Besides, this is something you must do alone. Benedicta will not harm you."

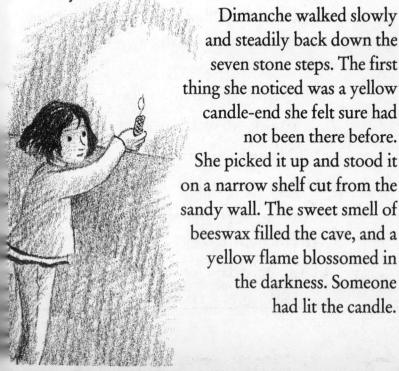

Dimanche walked slowly and steadily back down the seven stone steps. The first thing she noticed was a yellow candle-end she felt sure had not been there before. She picked it up and stood it on a narrow shelf cut from the sandy wall. The sweet smell of beeswax filled the cave, and a yellow flame blossomed in the darkness. Someone had lit the candle.

Dimanche stood still, waiting for Benedicta to appear. But instead of watching the steps, down which she expected the wise woman to come walking, perhaps with a basket of fish from the Fenny, she felt her eyes drawn irresistibly towards an arch of ferns that sprang from a corner of the cave. Had it been there before? Dimanche parted the ferns carefully. Behind them, a wooden box was hidden. In the bottom of the box lay a slip of wrinkled leather. Dimanche sighed happily. Benedicta was keeping her promise. This must be the Diller Deed.

Opening out the faded fragment of soft leather, Dimanche saw not the Diller Deed – but faint and spidery, in faded ink, these words:

If you in danger be,
Seek now the sea.
Sleeping nuns find,
Where grey tides wind
Round a forgotten isle.
Full fast and fierce the tide,
And wild the weather be.
Beware the sea.

Dimanche nodded, took the scrap of soft leather, folded it carefully, and put it back inside the box. She glanced round the cave, whispered a thank you, and blew out the flickering candle. Then she felt her way back up the dark steps to the waiting wood. Wolfie and Brother Betony were nowhere to be seen.

"If I must go to sea, I'll need my raft," Dimanche decided. Wishing there was some way she could let her aunt know what was going on, she set off for the boathouse. There was no time to stop and look for Wolfie.

Nine

The storm clouds frayed away to nothing, and the moon lit the way through the wood. In normal circumstances, Dimanche would never have taken her raft out on the river alone, not even in broad daylight, never mind by night, in stormy weather. She was far too sensible for that. But you must remember that her circumstances were far from normal. She picked up the paddle Wolfie had made her, pulled on her lifejacket, and set off.

Even though her situation was a desperate one, Dimanche could not help enjoying herself as her raft sped swiftly down the Fenny. In some places the current was strong enough to allow her to lean back, lift the paddle clear of the water, and go with the flow. Now and then a fish rose, spinning circles out across the water as it took a fly. Once a heron drifted out of the reeds, grey wings flapping in slow motion, long legs trailing.

Some miles below the mill, the river broadened, and the current slowed, and Dimanche began to paddle in earnest. Benedicta's rhyme went round and round inside her head in time to her own steady dip and splash.

If you in danger be,
Seek now the sea.

Well, I am, she thought, and I will. Thank you, Benedicta.

Presently the Fenny became a canal, and Dimanche skimmed through the little town of Rockford Market. She noticed the offices of Bludgeon & Bludgeon in Canal Walk, their windows dark. She glanced down at her watch. Four forty-five a.m. Nineteen and a quarter hours till midnight.

Town ducks quacked and quivered on the tow path. A tramp woman, wide awake and reading a book by the light of the moon, looked up and waved to Dimanche.

Then the town was behind her, the canal became a river once more, and Dimanche found herself gliding between flat fields full of dozing cows. There were caravans and trailers parked by the end of a bridge. A dog barked, and a young man, up to his knees in the river tickling trout, lifted his hat and winked as Dimanche paddled by.

Dimanche's back and shoulders were on fire with paddling. One narrow streak of yellow lit the east when she turned the last bend in the river and saw the estuary, grey-blue and shimmering with early sea lavender, spread out ahead of her. Mist smoked over the water, russet at first like the dawn, then apricot, then gold. It wrapped itself round her in a damp, white wall, encircling her raft. All beyond was silence, and stillness, and mist.

It's hard to tell, when you're cut off from all landmarks, if you are moving or standing still. Dimanche peered down into the water. It streamed away on either side of the raft as though a hidden hand had taken hold of the little vessel and was drawing it through the water. Which way was out? Which way was back? Impossible to tell.

Dimanche understood, then, just how foolish she had been. To paddle down the Fenny in the dead of night, telling nobody where she was going, was unwise. To set out across a mist-enshrouded estuary at dawn, heading for a forgotten island, broke all the rules of common sense.

Dimanche was not one to give up easily, but she was near to tears when, sometime towards midday, there was a scrape and a crunch and the raft shuddered to a halt, pitching her halfway over the side. She stared into the thick, soft, mist. Pearls of moisture dripped from her curly fringe down onto her eyelashes. She shook her head and rubbed her eyes. Two sharp rocks stuck up out of the water right beside her. The raft was grounded on the base of one of them, and breaking up fast. Dimanche tried in vain to jolt it free, rocked harder, heard a cracking, splintering sound, and felt the chill of water rising up her body.

No good sailor goes anywhere without a pack of flares. These powerful fireworks are invaluable for summoning help. When Dimanche first showed Verity her raft – which she'd built secretly, with Wolfie's help – Verity presented her with the flares, a life jacket with whistle attached, a compass, and a packet of emergency rations to be kept at all times in a tin box by the tiller. Making a desperate lunge for the flares, which were sealed in a waterproof wrapping, Dimanche threw herself over the side.

The sea was every bit as cold as she'd expected, but to her great surprise it hardly reached her waist. Just as her feet hit bottom, a tunnel opened in the mist, showing land close by. Either she had drifted back onshore, or else she'd found an island. Dimanche pulled the battered fragments of her raft up onto the beach, and looked around. The emergency rations were gone, but the flares were safe.

The island looked quite small. Tiny, in fact. It

was flat round the edges and rose to a point in the middle, rather like a pimple. Very like a pimple, Dimanche thought, staring at the pointy bit. Or like an island with a ruin in the middle of it.

The ruin was circular, and made of stone. It must once have had two storeys, but the upper storey had long since collapsed, leaving the old stone stairs to spiral up into the empty air. From the foot of the stairs, seaweedy steps led down into the earth. There must be an underground chamber, or a cellar, beneath the ruin. No. Probably not a cellar, Dimanche thought. Judging by the arched door and pointed windows, the ruin was a chapel. Or it had been. What would there be, underneath a chapel? A vault. A crypt. A place where nuns sleep.

Now, Dimanche was not a nervous person, but she could not, immediately, bring herself to go down into the crypt. Instead, she took off her lifejacket, and walked all round the tiny island. She was surprised to find it very wet. Almost as though it had been under water. When she had circled it several times, she sat down on the ground and began to chew a juicy grass stem. She was dreadfully thirsty. The grass stem didn't do much for her thirst, in fact it made it worse, but she was still sitting on the grass, chewing, when a power boat roared out of the morning mist. At the wheel of the power boat was the thin man.

Dimanche decided not to hide. It would be pointless and undignified. She stood up, and waited for him to approach.

Ten

The thin man did not look pleased to see Dimanche. His pale eyes glittered, and his thin lips twisted down into a sneer as he bent over the remains of the raft, cut open the packet of flares, and tossed them into the water. He watched them sink, picked up the lifejacket, and threw it out to sea. Then he turned to Dimanche.

"What are you doing here?" he asked. "You ought to be in Monks Wood with your fat fool of a friend!"

"What did you do to Wolfie?" Dimanche demanded. "Who are you? And why are you following me?"

"My name is Verdigris. *Professor* Verdigris. And I'm *not* following you. Why would a famous criminologist follow a stupid child? But since you're here, and all alone, I shall have to deal with you."

"I'm not alone. My aunt's got all my friends out searching for me."

Dimanche had no idea if this was true. But even

though she was very much afraid of the thin man, she could bluff, and she could hope, and she did both.

"Who cares about your friends? By the time they get here, the island will be gone."

"Islands don't disappear."

"This one does. When the moon is full, and the tide is high."

"That can't be true. No one would ever have lived here if it did. And people did live here, once."

"Indeed they did. The Wicked Sisters, they were called. Dreadful things happened here, they say." Verdigris smiled. He enjoyed dreadful things. "But the island sank, and the sea rose, long ago. I came here to collect something, not to waste my time on you. The dead sleep lightly on the island. I shall leave you in their hands."

"You can't do that! I'll drown!" And horrible though the professor was, Dimanche felt she would rather go with him, even as his prisoner, than be left alone on a sinking, haunted island.

"Yes, I rather think you will. And in a few hours – eleven, to be precise – your old home will be my property. Mine and my wife's." Verdigris smiled again, flashing his long, uneven teeth. "My wife knows your home. She has plans for it."

"What sort of plans?"

"We're going to turn it into a top-class boarding school. Private. Very private. Expensive, too. My wife has a brilliant head for business, and I'm an expert when it comes to bad behaviour. Between us we know exactly how to deal with obstinate, obtuse, interfering, ignorant, inconvenient children."

Professor Verdigris scuttled across the stony beach and grabbed Dimanche by the hair. He took a length of strong rope from his pocket and tied Dimanche up like a bluebottle in a spider's web. She fought as hard as she was able, and managed to land half a dozen good hard kicks on his bony shins. She might have bitten him, but she could not bring herself to try, because of the unpleasant smell and the damp, slightly shiny look of his skin.

He swore when she kicked him, and flapped at her with his long thin fingers, but he did not stop tying her up. When he was absolutely sure she couldn't move a finger, he carried her over to a tall, pointy rock which stood on the beach, sand to one side of it, sea to the other. Dimanche could tell by the colour of the water beyond the rock that the sea bed shelved steeply away. Professor Verdigris looped the last of the rope half a dozen times around the rock and knotted it efficiently.

When he had finished, he stood back, and bowed. His shiny shoes clicked against the pebbles of the beach. "High tide is at eleven," he said. Then he turned and loped across the short grass to the ruined chapel.

By turning her head and swivelling her eyes, Dimanche was able to watch him disappearing down the steps of the crypt. His shiny shoes, his legs, and half his skinny body had vanished, and only his skull-like head still showed above ground when, halfway down the steps, he stopped stock still. His cheeks turned green. His straggle of grey hair rose a fraction from his smooth and pointed skull. His mouth opened, but no sound came out. He put up his hands and fanned out his long, thin fingers, as if he were trying to push something cobwebby away from his face.

Professor Verdigris backed in slow motion up the steps, stopped at the top to stare down into the crypt for one more horrified moment, then ran.

He did not stop and he did not look back. He threw himself into his motor boat, switched on the powerful engine, and swept away in a white wash and a cloud of diesel fumes.

Eleven

Tied to the rock and unable to move, Dimanche waited for whatever it was that had so terrified the professor to come up the steps of the crypt and see her. However hard she strained to turn her head, she could see no more than the top step. Something might easily be standing halfway up and she would see nothing.

She kept absolutely still, and waited. Around her feet the water lapped and trickled, rolling the round grey pebbles of the beach this way and that. The tide was going down. How long had the professor said until it came back up? About ten hours, Dimanche thought. Moving only her eyeballs, she looked at her watch. It had stopped, because of being under water.

Into her exhausted brain crept a fragment of a childhood memory of song. She remembered Polly, leaning over her cot and singing to her. She seemed to hear part of that old song now . . .

Low, low, breathe and blow,
Wind of the western sea!
Over the rolling waters go,
Come from the dying moon, and blow . . .

A tear trickled down her cheek. She closed her weary eyes and, resting her chin on her knees as best she could, leaned back against the rock. The coils of rope pillowed her tired shoulders, and she fell into the sleep of deep exhaustion.

She dreamed of caves, and candlelight. She dreamed of Polly singing to her by the fire. She dreamed back, further back, of rocking in a hammock while the scent of lilac tickled her small round nose, and a bell rang softly in the distance.

When she woke it was evening, and the light was going. An icy wave swished round her ankles. Someone really was singing. The song was in Latin, so that Dimanche could not understand it, but it sounded like a song of friendship, a calling-in, almost a come-and-be-fed song. Dimanche turned her head as far as she could in each direction, but the singer remained hidden from her.

"Help!" she shouted. "Help! I'm here! Tied to this rock!"

Nothing happened. The singing went on.

Dimanche could actually feel the water rising up her shins. It's a terrible thing to be powerless at the mercy of the sea. She did not want to turn her head and look out at the hungry sea, but she could not stop herself.

The shock of what she saw made her jump so violently that she banged her chin on her knees and bit her tongue. There, in the deep water, just beyond the rock, watching her with an expression of benevolent curiosity, was a creature with a high forehead, a curving smile, and a gentle, knowing eye.

The dolphin looked a long look, deep into Dimanche's frightened eyes. His smile did not change – it was not, after all, really a smile, being simply the natural shape of his mouth. But his eyes held tenderness and pity.

"I think I'm going to die here," Dimanche told him. "If I am, I would like you to stay with me."

The dolphin whistled and submerged, leaving Dimanche lonelier and more terrified than she had been before he came. But the singing continued, chanting, enchanting, sliding in and out and all around Dimanche's troubled mind, while the water crept gradually up towards her knees and chin. She shivered and shook and her teeth chattered uncontrollably.

Not till the water was lapping at her chin did the dolphin return. Then he burst out of the water like a torpedo, clicking and whistling, soaking Dimanche's head and shoulders with a wash of bubbling green salt water.

He snapped up the frayed end of Verdigris's rope in his powerful beak, twirled it two or three times round his jaws, and headed out to sea. The rope cut him short immediately. He rose into the air like a flying cliff, fell back, and hit the water with a slap like a shotgun.

Dimanche shook her head at him. "You're only pulling the knots tighter," she said. "If you go on, you'll hurt yourself."

The dolphin ignored her, and repeated his experiment. Round on the landward side of the rock, above Dimanche's head, the rope pulled taut across a sharp piece of the rock. The dolphin tugged. The outer fibres of the rope began to fray. The dolphin tugged again. Dimanche shook her head. The rope frayed a little more. By the dolphin's fifth tug, two of the three strands of the rope were cut right through. On his next attempt, they parted with a twang. A hank of wet rope fell across Dimanche's face, the dolphin leapt clear of the water in a triple somersault of triumph, and Dimanche began to wriggle herself free.

The singing died away. The dolphin vanished. Dimanche turned from the cold waves that lapped the beach towards the centre of the island. No singer was visible, but Dimanche knew now where the voice had come from, and what she must do next.

Twelve

She forced herself to walk towards the ruined chapel. She had known all along, really, that the Deed and Title would be in the crypt. A low moan came and went from beneath the chapel floor, together with a rattling scrape as old and dry as a desert. Dimanche shivered. But unlike the professor, she did not run.

Whatever it was that scared Professor Verdigris away, she told herself, it has not come after me. It could have got me any time. I've been tied to a rock, asleep, for hours and hours, and it hasn't done a thing. Maybe it can't come out of the crypt. Maybe it can only get you if you go down the steps.

If anyone is buried down there, Dimanche thought, it will only be nuns. Nuns are mostly good people. Like Aunt Verity. I expect you get the odd mean one. Some of them are probably quite strict and bossy. But very few would actually be wicked. So neither would their ghosts be. Brother Betony is a ghost and I wasn't scared of him.

Benedicta's ghost came into the cave and lit the candle, and I wasn't scared of her. Somebody's ghost just called a dolphin out of the sea to set me free. What am I frightened of?

The moan became a rustle, then a sigh.

Dimanche thought about Tom Shovel, the Hilton in the Hollow gravedigger. He lived in a cabin beside the graveyard, and he was not afraid of dead people. "Dead people never hurt nobody," he used to tell Dimanche, when she was little, and frightened of the grave stones. "Not like live people. Live people can be proper mean. But don't you worry your head about dead ones. They ain't interested in you nor me. Most likely they've got other fish to fry."

Benedicta promised to help any Diller who should be in direst need, Dimanche told herself. She is on my side. She told me to find the sleeping nuns. She wouldn't send me where it wasn't safe to go.

Dimanche looked out to sea. The rolling tide was washing up towards the ruined chapel. Most of the island was already under water.

Down she went, into the crypt. It was darker below ground than above it, but Dimanche could just make out two rows of sarcophagi facing one another in silent tranquillity across a clean stone floor.

The moaning sound came from the whorled spiral of a sea shell which lay on the second step, catching the breeze off the sea, turning it into sea songs. Further down, hanging like a tattered banner from a high stone gable, a ribbon of seaweed scraped and rattled as the wind brushed it against a rough stone pillar.

Dimanche bent to read the inscription on the nearest sarcophagus. It said *Sister Septuagesima ~ Mercifully Delivered in the Year of Our Lord…* the rest of the writing was worn away. Beside Sister Septuagesima lay Sister Catherine, and beside her Sister Araminta, then Sister Aspasia and then Sister Chloe.

"If it was you who called the dolphin, Sister Septuagesima, thank you," Dimanche said politely. "And if it was you who chased off the professor, thank you for that as well. And Sister Catherine and Sister Araminta and Sister Aspasia and Sister Chloe. And I'm sorry to disturb you. But Professor Verdigris has hidden my Deed and Title down here. And Benedicta sent me to get it back. I think."

No one answered. Nothing moved. The silent sepulchres were silent still, as they had been for centuries.

A heavy metal strongbox, the sort you might find

in a bank vault, lay on the lid of Sister Septuagesima's sarcophagus. The key was still in the lock. Dimanche turned it and lifted the lid. Inside, wrapped in oilskin, lay the Diller Deed and Title. Carefully, Dimanche undid a corner and began to read:

We ~ the King's men ~ do most solemnly proclaim ~ this being the Year of Our Lord MLXXXVI ~ that Hilton Halle in the fair Vale of Hilton shall be and remain the home of King William's loved and loyal subject Decimus Deodatus Diller.

It shall from this day hence be house and home to all his kith and kin ~ for as long as Dillers shall preserve this Royal Proclamation.

Furthermore they shall ~ each and every one hundred years ~ at Midsummer Midnight ~ show this Royal Proclamation to whichsoever men of law ~ dwelling close by the Halle ~ demand to see it.

If any Diller fail to show this Royal Proclamation to the appointed men of law on the appointed hour ~ ~ ~ then House ~ Hall ~ Woods ~ Goods ~ Serfs ~ Chattels and Appurtenances ~ including children ~ shall pass into the hand of any man or woman who can show the Proclamation at the appointed hour.

~ signed ~ ~ ~ 𝔚𝔦𝔩𝔩𝔦𝔞𝔪 ~ ~

Dimanche said thank you again to Sister Septuagesima, wrapped the Deed and Title up inside its oilskin cover, and stuffed it inside her T-shirt, which was firmly tucked into the waistband of her trousers.

Thirteen

Dimanche's stomach felt as if it had shrunk into a little acorn. It pressed against her backbone in a cramping, won't-stop ache. She was not sure how long she could live without food, but her hunger was mild compared to her thirst. It made her brain throb and her throat burn and her skin prickle as though she had a fever – which, in fact, she very soon had.

The tide was rising fast as Dimanche collected the fragments of her raft and made a rapid search for driftwood. She found two planks, three branches, one log, part of a wooden pallet, and eight plastic bags. There was wire round the pallet, not much, but strong. She cut her hand and broke a nail trying to get it off the pallet, and it hurt her hands to wind it round the planks and branches, but before long she had another raft of sorts. It was held together at one end by wire and at the other by torn-up plastic bags. If it came apart, which looked pretty likely, Dimanche hoped to survive by clinging tightly to the largest of the bits of wood.

Unless of course the tide turned while she was adrift. If that happened, she would be swept out to sea. Meanwhile, on every side the sea poured in. It filled the estuary, ridged waves flowing in never-ending lines towards the land, lapping, nibbling, here bunching and rushing in strange watery contortions, there flat, with horrid dimples showing where the undertow would drag down anything it caught. Dimanche knew that she would be in deadly danger, alone on a makeshift raft in the coming boil of cross-currents. But what choice had she?

Perhaps you think that she was foolish even to think of setting out across the high tide, in the dark, on a cobbled-up raft? Perhaps you think she should have waited to see if the tide was really going to cover the whole island? Perhaps she should have. But remember, if she didn't get home by midnight, with the Deed and Title, she wouldn't *have* a home. I must go now, she thought, and take my chance.

In the midst of these alarming thoughts, one troubling phrase from the Deed and Title kept returning to Dimanche's mind ... *House ~ Halle ~*

Woods ~ Goods ~ Serfs ~ Chattels and Appurtenances ~ including children ~ shall pass into the hand of any who can show the Proclamation at the appointed hour.

What did that mean, exactly? Dimanche wondered. It sounded very much as though she herself might fall into the hands of the professor and his mysterious wife – whoever *she* might be. Dimanche remembered all too well how terrible it was to be in the power of someone wicked.

Some people panic in this kind of situation. Others give up hope. Dimanche did neither. She finished her raft and dragged it down to the water. With great care, and while the raft was still in shallow water, she climbed aboard, spreading her weight evenly so as not to tip it up. She hesitated, staring out into the estuary, where the waves already churned like boiling porridge. Then, using both hands, she paddled slowly out into deep water.

The raft bobbed and jostled and gradually floated clear of the grassy bank. Dimanche held tightly to the largest of the logs. The cry of a curlew bubbled out across the sunset. Dimanche wondered if Sister Septuagesima had heard the same sound, long ago. What had it been like, she wondered, to live on such a tiny island?

Then the tide took her, and twirled her round, and nudged her away from the shore. The little raft rocked, and the waves splashed, and Dimanche knew that, for better or worse, she was on her way.

Far to the west the sun sank among tiger stripes of red and gold. The island was hidden under water. Only the old stone chapel stood clear above the waves. Sister Septuagesima's sepulchre lay now beneath the salty sea; fishes swam in and out of the chapel windows.

The raft shifted under Dimanche and the waves grew rougher. One after another, the twisted ropes she'd made from torn-up plastic bags began to pull taut, rip, and unravel. The planks and branches parted. Dimanche slid through into the suck and slap of the sea's icy swirl.

She tried her hardest to haul herself up so she could sit astride the largest of the logs. Time and again she heaved herself half over the log, balancing on her stomach, her chin just clear of the water, but every time she swung her leg up, the log rolled under her, and back she fell. The continuous struggle, combined with the fear and the cold, was too much for her. She longed for the wide smile of the dolphin, and his steady eye, but in her heart she knew he would not come unless the sleeping sisters called him. Very soon all that she could do was hang on, and hope.

She had been doing this for some time, and was beginning to find both quite difficult, when she heard the thrum of a small engine. It came from the direction of the land, and seemed to be heading straight towards the island. It sounded just like Cosmo's lawn mower. I've gone delirious, Dimanche thought. Which probably means I'm going to die.

Then she realised where the noise was coming from. She turned her eyes upwards, and what she saw convinced her that her mind was wandering. High in the sky, buzzing like a mosquito, a black speck pottered towards the far horizon like a tiny iron filing drawn by the magnet of the sunset's fading glow.

Dimanche took one arm from the log to shade her eyes, tipped back her head until the water tugged her curly hair, and gazed into the limpid sky. The black speck hung still for a second, sputtering, then turned and circled back around the estuary.

As it came closer, Dimanche saw it was a small mono-plane. It had a single large propeller at the front, two pram wheels dangling like duck's feet from its belly, and a banner streaming from the cockpit. This was open to the sky, so that Dimanche could see the pilot, sitting in a deck chair, his round face half-hidden by his mighty hunter hat and goggles, his large hands gripping the joystick, his mouth wide open as he sang with the joy of a man born to fly.

"Wolfie!" she shouted, letting go with the other hand and waving wildly. "Wolfie! I'm down here!"

Wolfie could not hear her above the *put put* of the engine, and the whirring of the propellers, and the buffeting of the wind, but he could see a tiny ant-like dot clinging to a twig adrift on the tide, and he knew at once that it was Dimanche.

"Hold on!" he yelled. "I'm comin' down!"

The mono-plane began a dipping, dancing descent, lower and lower over the water. Soon Dimanche could see Wolfie's beefy hand waving over the side of the cockpit, making a thumbs-up, *everything's-gonna-be-OK* sign.

Neither Wolfie nor Dimanche noticed Professor Verdigris's power boat speeding towards them across the choppy water.

Fourteen

Hope filled the professor's cowardly heart as he sped towards Dimanche. He had watched with anger and amazement as the dolphin set her free. He had held his breath as she went down into the crypt. He had watched her come back up, alive, patch together a new raft, and put to sea. Then, as the sea grew rougher, he had lost her. Now is my moment! he thought, when he saw her again, bobbing in the water. She's got the Deed! She must have! All I have to do is ram her and grab it. I'll leave her to drown and still reach Hilton Hall by midnight.

At that point he realised that he'd better hurry, because whoever was flying the small plane that had appeared from nowhere seemed to have the same idea.

If the professor had carried a gun, my story would end here, because he could easily have picked off Wolfie and Dimanche, and left the bodies for the fish. The tide would have washed Dimanche's pathetic raft bits up onto the shore, where they would have looked like nothing more than driftwood. Wolfie's wonderful machine would have been lost for ever under the sea.

But the professor hadn't got a gun. "Certainly not, Verdigris," his wife had told him when he'd said he ought to have one. "You'd probably shoot yourself."

When the professor spotted Dimanche bobbing in the water, he was torn between hope and amazement. Hope, that she might have got the Deed and Title. Amazement, that neither the tide nor the terror of the crypt had got her. She might have got it, he thought. I bet she's got it. A child who escapes from five metres of rope knotted round a rock, and the Wicked Sisters, and the high tide, will not have left the Deed behind. I'll ram her log and grab the Deed. I can still reach Hilton Hall by midnight. But that interfering brat will not reach it at all.

The professor had forgotten that it is not always wise to count your hens before they're hatched.

Wolfie and Dimanche spotted the professor at the same time. Wolfie dived low over Dimanche. When he was hanging just above her, fanning the waves to frothing mountains, he threw out a rope. Dimanche grabbed it, wound it round her middle twice, knotted it and waved to Wolfie. He began to winch her in. For a few, breathtaking moments she swung, suspended between sea and sky like a spider on a thread. Then Wolfie hauled her into the cockpit.

At first the plane seemed unable to rise above sea level, its tiny motor struggling with the extra weight of Dimanche and her sodden clothes. Professor Verdigris, guessing as much, opened up the throttle on his power boat and hurtled, like a deadly arrow, straight at the struggling mono-plane.

Although he did not have a gun, Professor Verdigris did have a harpoon. Aiming carefully from the rocking boat for Wolfie's undercarriage, he gently squeezed the trigger. There was a quiet pop, and half a league of rope uncoiled across the water. The head of the harpoon buried itself in Wolfie's throbbing fuselage, pierced his sandwich box and stuck fast in his thermos flask, which exploded, showering his feet with boiling cocoa.

Dimanche, who was half-mad with thirst, began to cry.

"Don't fret, Dimanche," Wolfie comforted. "I brought us a bottle of ginger beer. You drink that, we could do with lightenin' the plane."

Joyfully, Dimanche drank deep draughts of icy ginger beer. This did not, of course, lighten the plane. But it made Dimanche feel quite wonderful.

Meanwhile, boat and plane, still joined by rope and harpoon, struggled like two terrified animals pulling in opposite directions. Wolfie relied on cautious, steady pressure. Verdigris, never a patient man, put his engine into reverse and turned the power up to maximum. Black smoke poured out, a flash of fire shot from his exhaust, and his powerful engine burst into flames.

Wolfie leaned far out of the plane and, with one swipe of his mighty hunter sheath knife, severed the rope, which fell back like a tired serpent into the sea. With a supreme effort, the little engine of Cosmo's lawn mower hauled the plane and its passengers up above the waves into the evening sky. Far below, Professor Verdigris doused the flames – he wasn't short of water – and began to row towards the mainland.

The plane soon left the estuary behind and, following the bright thread of the Fenny, began to chug steadily upriver towards Hilton in the Hollow. Shadows of the evening stretched velvet curtains behind every hill, filling the valleys with dusk, while the hilltops shone in the last light of evening. Sheep the size of daisy petals, cows and horses like toy farm animals, barking dogs, rabbits like soft full stops, and minute, invisible mice, all heard the plane pass over, paused for a moment, and continued their munching, hunting, dreaming lives.

Wolfie could not resist showing off a bit. He swooped low over sleepy villages to bring the children tumbling out of doors, panting and pointing in excited pleasure as the little plane sped past, its banner streaming behind it. Soft as a moth against the deepening blue of the night sky, sharp as a bat against the harvest moon, it was a sight none of them was ever to forget.

The small plane circled the hilltops, and floated down into the river valleys. Wolfie could not speak for joy. Beside him, Dimanche gazed, enraptured, at the countryside. It looked so right somehow, seen from the sky. For the first time in her life, her body was moving almost as fast as her eye and her brain. She did not notice, and neither did Wolfie, the headlights of a fast car speeding along the country roads beneath them.

"Wolfie," Dimanche bellowed presently. "How did you know where to find me?"

"Benedicta told me."

"You mean you saw her? And she spoke to you?"

Wolfie nodded. "That's two ghosts I've spoke to. And they was both nice people."

"When I came out of the cave you were gone, Wolfie, and so was Brother Betony. Where did you go?"

"I dunno where I went. I saw people wearin' funny clothes, and monks all singin'."

"I thought you'd been knocked out."

"I was. Benedicta made me better."

After that they gave up talking, it was too difficult above the noisy engine. In less than half an hour, Hilton Hall appeared, moonlit, nestling in the sheltering bowl of Hilton valley. The village dozed beside it and the river, now a stream, wound away into the shadows of Monks Wood. Below them, still unnoticed, the fast car sped towards Hilton Hall.

Fifteen

The old front door of Hilton Hall was open. Someone stood waiting on the stone steps that led down to the gravel drive. Someone who brought back dreadful memories for Dimanche. Memories of fear, and loneliness, and sorrow, of shouting, and anger, and long hours locked in a dark attic. Someone cruel and cunning.

Verity Victorine and Polly Cockle came pelting out of the back door when they heard the plane. Chief Superintendent Barry Bullpit was already hurrying up the lane that led from the station. Puffing along behind him were two stout figures who paused to stare up at the night sky in astonishment. Baldwin and Bartholomew Bludgeon, Dimanche guessed. She glanced at her watch. There were four minutes till midnight.

The little plane circled the meadow and dipped behind the hawthorn hedge. The woman waiting on the steps frowned angrily. There should not be a plane. A fast car, yes. A small plane, no.

She felt so sure her planning had been faultless. Twice before, she had tangled with Dimanche Diller. Twice before, Dimanche had beaten her. This time, nothing could go wrong. This time, she had planned everything perfectly, down to the smallest detail.

"*Brainwiddle*!" she muttered angrily. "Come here *at once*!"

Verdigris's wife had been a guest in Her Majesty's Prison The Vaults, at Wold-under-Water, when she met and fell for the professor. He was a famous criminologist, and he was studying the effect on criminals of being locked up. As far as he could tell, it seemed to be affecting them in much the same way as it does other people – badly. Prisoner number 4723 did not at first sight cause the professor's heart to melt, and neither did his scrawny body, nor his peculiar smell, immediately bowl her over. But love took its course, as it will no matter what the circumstances, and when prisoner number 4723's sentence was up, she married her professor. Deep in her greedy brain a plan was hatching. A plan to rob Dimanche, once and for all, of everything she possessed.

She planned the break-in that allowed Professor Verdigris to search Verity's study. She sent him up into the attic, where he discovered the whereabouts of the Deed and Title, as well as the location of Nuns' Island. Next came the robbery of the Rockford Market bank. Standing on the old stone steps of Hilton Hall waiting for her hour of triumph, the professor's wife congratulated herself heartily. The brain work, the planning, the forethought, the scrupulous attention to detail, all had been hers. So should the prize be. This time she had overlooked nothing. (Except, just possibly, three ghosts, a dolphin, Wolfie T. Volfango's powers of invention, and Dimanche Diller's courage.)

"It will be *mine!*" she cried. "*All* of it! I *deserve* it!"

Dimanche tumbled out of Wolfie's plane and dashed across the meadow to the foot of the steps.

"Oh do you, Valburga Vilemile?" she shouted. "I don't think so!"

"Who cares what *you* think, you pathetic little pustule?" Valburga Vilemile jeered. "There are precisely sixty seconds till midnight! Verdigris has got the Deed and Title! In sixty seconds all this will be *mine*! Including you, you miserable appurtenance!"

"How dare you say such things, you wicked, wicked woman?" Verity cried, hurling herself in a flurry of coif and habit at Valburga.

It was at this moment that Professor Verdigris screeched to a halt in a shower of gravel. He spotted Barry Bullpit, guessed that the game was up, crashed his gears into reverse, and sped off backwards down the drive.

"Verdigris, you cowardly weasel! Come back this instant! How dare you leave me here?" roared his wife.

Verdigris froze for a moment, caught in his wife's anger like a rabbit in the glare of a car's headlights. In that moment Chief Superintendent Barry Bullpit snapped a pair of handcuffs round his scrawny wrists, attaching him securely to the steering wheel of his car. Using his spare pair of cuffs he attached

Valburga to her trembling husband. Then he pocketed the car keys and strolled indoors to telephone for reinforcements.

"Ten seconds till midnight," announced Bartholomew and Baldwin Bludgeon, in unison. "Has anyone here present got the Deed and Title?"

Dimanche pulled a sodden ball of inky parchment from under her jumper.

"*Yes!*" she shouted. "I have! Bad luck, Valburga Vilemile! I've beaten you again!"

Baldwin and Bartholomew Bludgeon took the sodden document from Dimanche and spread it out upon the grass as best they could. By the light of Papa Fettler's lantern – he had arrived while Barry Bullpit was restraining Valburga Vilemile – they verified its authenticity.

"All in order, though a trifle damp," they told Dimanche. "Now, what about the brandy?"

Sixteen

It was long after midnight, in fact it was nearly dawn, when Dimanche finally got to bed. She had enjoyed the Victory Supper, especially the two whole bottles of elderflower cordial, but it would be a long time before she forgot what thirst, real thirst, feels like. Unseen among the guests, Benedicta and Brother Betony drank her health in Hilton Valley Velvet. One thing, and one thing only, cast a shadow on the celebrations. It had to do with Wolfie T. Volfango. And it was very nearly tragic.

When Dimanche scrambled out of the plane and rushed across the lawn to confront her old enemy, Valburga Vilemile, Wolfie stayed behind, hidden from sight in the cockpit. He had important reasons for avoiding Chief Superintendent Barry Bullpit. As he crouched in the cockpit with his large nose pressed against the control panel, a powerful whiff of petrol made him want to sneeze.

The engine didn't ought to smell like that, thought Wolfie, sniffing. Later on, when everyone's asleep, I'll strip it down and see what's leakin'. He decided to head for the potting shed and have a nap while he waited for everyone to go indoors.

Sometimes the very best things happen just by luck, and Wolfie's decision to leave the plane and hide in the potting shed was one of those.

He stepped out of the cockpit and strolled thoughtfully away towards the kitchen garden, taking care to keep himself well hidden in the shadows. He paused by the wall for a final glance back at his pride and joy. And that was when he saw it.

A curling, furling wisp of black smoke trailed up from the open cockpit. It grew into a cloud, a curtain, a dense and oily black excretion. Soot showered upwards, there was a heavy thud, and Wolfie's precious plane erupted in a ball of roaring red flame.

He had built the machine of his dreams. As it burned, Wolfie cried bitter tears. Dimanche, hearing the explosion, and guessing at once what it must be, leapt from the table and shot across the lawn towards the flames. If Wolfie was inside that red inferno, she would get him out or die.

Wolfie saw her coming, launched himself, and brought her down with a flying tackle just as the burning plane exploded like a firework, throwing out jets of flame and jagged bits of red hot metal in all directions. Wolfie and Dimanche rolled over and over, finally coming to rest in Cosmo's herb garden. Gradually the sweet scent of crushed mint blotted out the stench of burning plane.

"I'm sorry about your plane, Wolfie," Dimanche said, presently. "Really, really sorry."

Midsummer moonlight silvered Wolfie's round bald head. His small eyes twinkled.

"Shucks, Dimanche," he replied. "It don't matter."

"Wolfie! It does!"

"Nope, Dimanche. It don't. You're safe. I'm safe. Valburga and Verdigris are beat. I'm sorry about Cosmo's lawn mower, of course I am. I was gonna put the motor back. But your auntie can buy another one. And if I built one plane, Dimanche, what's gonna stop me from buildin' another? Better than the first?"

Dimanche smiled. "Nothing is, Wolfie," she said. "Nothing is."

DIMANCHE DILLER
by Henrietta Branford

Smarties Book Prize Winner
Shortlisted for the Guardian Award

"What children want is squashing down! What children want is flattening out!"

Would you want a guardian who said that? Dimanche Diller certainly didn't, but she had one anyway – called Valburga Vilemile! And Valburga has more than a squashing planned for Dimanche. After all, it's only Dimanche who stands in the way of what Valburga wants above everything else – Hilton Hall and the Diller family fortune. But Dimanche isn't easy to defeat – so who will flatten who?

"A galloping story of escape and adventure." *Guardian*

DIMANCHE DILLER
IN DANGER
by Henrietta Branford

Am safe and well but have been captured.
Try not to worry.
Love,
Dimanche.

Dimanche thought she had beaten her old enemy
Valburga Vilemile, who's gone to prison. But
locking Valburga up hasn't made her lose her evil
cunning – her new plan to kidnap Dimanche and
hold her to ransom is horribly successful.
Valburga has enlisted her nephew, Wolfie, to carry
out the dreadful deed, and this time Dimanche's
friend Polly is not around to save her.

A whizz-bang new adventure to follow the
Smarties Prize-winning *Dimanche Diller*!

Order Form

To order direct from the publishers, just make a list of the titles you want and fill in the form below:

Name ....

Address ....

....

....

Send to: Dept 6, HarperCollins Publishers Ltd, Westerhill Road, Bishopbriggs, Glasgow G64 2QT.

Please enclose a cheque or postal order to the value of the cover price, plus:

UK & BFPO: Add £1.00 for the first book, and 25p per copy for each addition book ordered.

Overseas and Eire: Add £2.95 service charge. Books will be sent by surface mail but quotes for airmail despatch will be given on request.

A 24-hour telephone ordering service is available to Visa and Access card holders: 0141-772 2281